J.C. Comes to Town

J.C. Comes to Town

Author:
Patrice Chambers

Illustrator:
Natalie Morino

XULON PRESS

Xulon Press
2301 Lucien Way #415
Maitland, FL 32751
407.339.4217
www.xulonpress.com

Printed in the United States of America.

ISBN-13: 9781545624548

MEANWHILE ON EARTH

Two Weeks Later...

34

 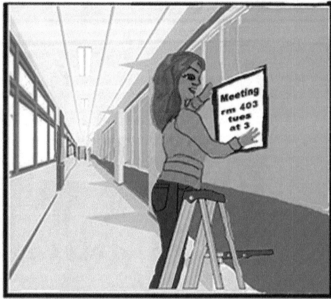

45

What Would J.C. Do?

Sometimes, we all need a little guidance. J.C. is here to guide you through some of those places in life where you might need a little help.

What would J.C. do if he were feeling down?

Let's just face it, being a Christian doesn't mean that you will always be happy. Sometimes you may find yourself a little down or even depressed. Does this make you a bad Christian or even a bad person? No!

What does the bible say? There are lots of instances in the bible that mentions people being depressed. You know Job, the guy that decided it was a good idea to run from God's calling on this life, found himself depressed and feeling like he was dying in Job 30:16. In Psalms 143, David asks the Lord to come quickly and answer him for his depression deepens. He felt like if the Lord turned away from him that he would die.

J.C. would do what he does best. He would talk to his heavenly father, make the necessary life changes that God is requiring of him, and then go and speak to a mental healthcare professional. Remember, we were never meant to walk this life alone. Invite someone in, when you need help.

What would J.C. do if he were overwhelmed?

Schoolwork, home life, parents, friendships, relationships, and other responsibilities… Sometimes this can all get overwhelming.

What does the bible say? In Mark 1:35 and Mark 6:31, the bible speaks of Jesus being overwhelmed by the crowds. They wanted so much from him that he didn't even have time to eat or rest! Jesus had to remove himself from these situations so that he would have time to commune with God.

Jesus's escapes from his overwhelming situations sometimes required him to be with his disciples, but sometimes he needed to be alone with just God. J.C. would decide if this was a situation that requires one-on-one time with God or if those that he had chosen to participate in life with could join. He would also take a serious look at the things that are overwhelming him. Are these things essential? Are these things apart of God's purpose for his life? Can organization help him to feel less overwhelmed? Who in my life can help me so I feel less overwhelmed. When all else fails… STOP, PRAY, and LISTEN!

What would J.C. do if he weren't getting along with his parents?

Sometimes, you may feel as though your parents just don't understand you. They were definitely born an adult, right? They were never your age. They could never see things from your point of view. Or could they?

What does the bible say? The bible gives parents and children very definite directives. In Proverbs 22:6, the bible tells parents to train up a child in a way that he should go and when he is old he will not depart from it. Your parents are tasked with training you in this scripture. Parents are told to discipline their children, if they love them in Proverbs 13:24. Being a parent is tough. You have to make sure you make the right decisions, in order to help your children, grow up to be who God has called them to be.

The bible tells children to honor their father and mother, so that they can live a long life in Exodus 6 and 20. It also says in Philippians 2:14 to "Do all things without grumbling or questioning." Translation: Don't talk back! Self-control is very hard! I understand.

J.C. would do his best to honor his mother and his father, because that's what God told him to do.

Both parties have a very difficult task, parents have to provide for a train their children in the way that God wants them to. Children have to be obedient and operate in self-control when dealing with their parents. Understanding the burden that both parties have to bear should bring about some love and understanding.

What would J.C. do if he weren't getting along with other family members?

Parents aren't the only family members that we encounter. There are brothers and sisters, aunts and uncles, grandparents, and even cousins that we have figure out how to deal with all of these people.

What does the bible say? In Genesis 3 and 4, we find the story of Cain and Abel. In the story, the Lord asks Cain for the whereabouts of his brother, Abel. Cain replies with, "I do not know. Am I my brother's keeper?" Cain had actually murdered his brother and caused a curse on the Earth, which caused the Earth not to grow his crops. Cain was guilty of not loving his brother the way that God intended for him to which resulted in his death.

Ok, so that example is a little extreme. Most of us are not going that far, but the bible also says in Mark 12:31, that we should love our neighbor as ourselves. Your neighbor does not have to live across the street, they could live in the room right next to yours. You may not call them your neighbor. You might call them your annoying little brother.

We saw J.C. deal with everyone he interacted with love. It was important for him to show God's love to all. This is our command whether we are dealing with family members or strangers.

What would J.C. do if he were scared?

We all deal with fear. Fear could be that feeling that you get when you go to a new school. It could also be making sure the lights are on when you enter a room after watching a horror movie. There is definitely guidance in the bible for dealing with fear.

What does the bible say? In 2ⁿᵈ Timothy 1:7, the bible says that fear was not given to us by God. In Isaiah 41:10, we are told that we don't have to fear because God is with us. He also promised to be our strength in this same verse.

J.C. would trust in God. Fully trusting in and loving God allows us to live without fear. If you know that God is always watching out for you, keeping you from all hurt, harm, and danger. What is there to be afraid of?

What would J.C. do if someone approached him about drugs?

There are a lot of things that are really not good for us floating around. One of them is drugs. Drugs can hurt your body and damage your mind. How do you avoid becoming a victim of drugs? How do you say no?

What does the bible say? Ok, so drug use isn't specifically mentioned in the bible, but in several places in the bible, we are commanded to "respect and obey the laws of the land." We are also told to be good stewards over everything that God has given to us, including our bodies in Matthew 25: 13-30. Damaging it with drugs is not being a good steward.

J.C. would say no. Other people's thoughts about him are not more important than what God has told him to do!

If you are tempted, find someone to talk to about it. Whether it be an adult or a friend that has also vowed to be a good steward over his or her body.

What would J.C. do if his grades were slipping?

When J.C. met Matt, he was sitting at a table overwhelmed by all of the things that he had to do in order to maintain his grades. He really cared about his grades and doing his best? He cared so much that he was completely stressed out. How do we do our best without becoming overwhelmed and letting things, like grades, slip?

What does the bible say? In Colossians 3:23-24 the bible says that whatever we do, we should do it as if we are doing it for the Lord. That's means doing everything in excellence. We are also called to be examples in speech, conduct, love, faith, and purity. That means always doing your best.

Sometimes things can get a little overwhelming and your grades can slip. J.C. would pray and ask God to lead him to the correct people to help him. He may need someone to help him get organized. Someone may be needed to help understand concepts presented in class. Remember to ask for help when you need it! Never suffer in silence!

What would J.C. do if he were being bullied?

People can be mean. Sometimes that meanness translates into bullying. So, what do you do if you are being bullied?

What does the bible say? In Deuteronomy 32:35, God states that vengeance belongs to him. This means that we are not called to fight our own battles, because God fights for us. In Deuteronomy 31:6, we are told to "Be strong and courageous and no to be in fear or dread, because God goes with us. Matthew 5:44 tells us to love our enemies and pray for those who persecute us.

Following those verses, may be easier said than done. J.C. may also find it difficult to love someone that is bullying him, but he would be obedient. Praying for enemies is one way to show love. J.C. would also seek help from an adult. There is no reason to go through this alone. Something can be done about it.

What would J.C. do if someone close to him died?

Death is a part of life, but that doesn't mean that it doesn't hurt. How should those that are left behind deal with death.

What does the bible say? According to 2 Corinthians 5:6-8, even when someone dies, we should "be of good courage," because to be "away from the body is to be at home with the lord."

It is our job to make sure that this is true for all of those that we love, so J.C. would make sure to be a witness to all that he knew of the love of God. He would make sure speak to as many people about God and a relationship with God as possible, so that when they are absent from their body, they would be present with the Lord.

CPSIA information can be obtained
at www.ICGtesting.com
Printed in the USA
LVOW05s2246220218
567619LV00005B/52/P

9 781545 624548